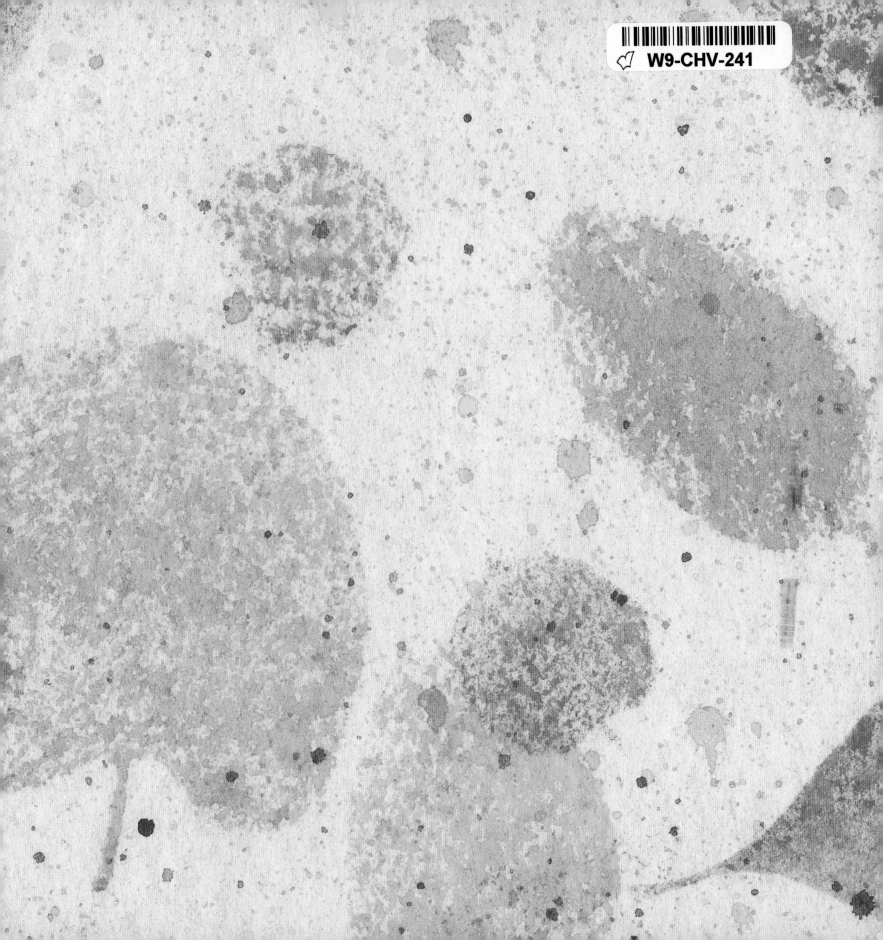

For
Stephen,
Mum, Dad & Jim

First published in 2013 by Child's Play (International) Ltd
Ashworth Road, Bridgemead, Swindon SN5 7YD UK

Published in USA by Child's Play Inc
250 Minot Avenue, Auburn, Maine 04210

Distributed in Australia by Child's Play Australia Pty Ltd
Unit 10/20 Narabang Way, Belrose, NSW 2085

ISBN 978-1-84643-595-9
CLP220113CPL03135959

Printed and bound in Shenzhen, China

1 3 5 7 9 10 8 6 4 2

A catalogue record of this book
is available from the British Library

www.childs-play.com

It's Not Yours,
IT'S MINE!

Susanna Moores

Blieka has a ball.

It's big, it's round—
and it's all Blieka's!

The ball was a present.

Oh, how Blieka loved the new toy!

Forever and always mine,
thought Blieka.

Blieka's friends kept
asking to borrow the ball.

Blieka told them every time,
"It's not yours..."

Blieka was worried.
Someone might take
the toy without asking.
So Blieka took it
EVERYWHERE.

To school...

...to the ocean...

...to the park.

To the pool...

...to the shop.

To the country...

...and even to
circus school.

One day,
Blieka noticed
the ball looked
different.

Blieka needed help.

Two friends came to the rescue.
SUCCESS!
So Blieka decided to give
sharing a try.

At first, Blieka found it quite hard.

But it got easier.

Well, a bit easier.

Word spread that Blieka
was sharing the ball.
And then, something
rather surprising happened.

Everyone brought
their toys to share too!